AF674207

The Tomb on The Hill

Sandali Anuradha

NARENDRA EDUX PUBLICATIONS

This is a work of fiction. Names, characters, places, and incidents are products of the author's imagination or are used fictitiously.

NARENDRA EDUX
PUBLICATIONS

Narendra EduX Publications

Address: Harari Bhita Tol, Post Baskhora, Thana Marauna, District

Supaul (Bihar)- 852133

Email:narendraedux@gmail.com

WhatsApp: +918521338895

This book is dedicated to my Parents, who gave me more than just love—they gave me the world through the thousands of books they placed in my hands. Every word I write is an echo of the endless support you have shown my dreams.

And to Narendra Yadav, my best friend, who saw the value in this story when it was hidden away. Thank you for being the strength I needed to finally bring this dream to life.

“Some bonds are not broken by the soil, but rooted deeper within it.”

In the quiet shadow of a lone oak tree, a secret remains buried, guarded by a girl whose face is half-hidden and a heart that refuses to forget.

When Anne Mary Anderson arrives at the magnificent Anderson Bungalow in Yorkshire, she finds a house full of servants, cold mists, and a heavy silence. But outside, on a lonely hill, stands a tomb that holds a secret story of past.

Who is the girl hidden from the world? What really happened during the tragic fire of the past? And why does the head housekeeper, Sarah Manson, look at Anne with such hidden malice?

In a world of sacrifice and silent endurance, some secrets are meant to be uncovered... and some bonds are essential to existence.

Content

Chapter 1

A new arrival

This story begins in a small rural village in Yorkshire. It is another narrative that explores how powerful the bonds formed within the human heart truly are, and how it is nearly impossible to say goodbye to a bond that has become essential to one's existence.

It was a busy day for all the servants working at Anderson Bungalow. Situated far from the small houses of the village, at the foot of a mountain ridge, this magnificent bungalow was rarely visited by its true owners. Mr. Jonathan Anderson, the current owner, was serving as a Governor in India. However, suddenly turning everything upside down, his only daughter arrived at the bungalow, following her father's orders.

Her father's intention was clear: this ancient, historic bungalow was the most suitable place for his only daughter to stay.

"Hey! Martha, be careful when you wipe that picture! And Sophie, go up to the kitchen and see if everything is ready for the meal!"

Sarah Manson, the head housekeeper, was busy barking orders at everyone. Despite her commanding presence, there was a visible restlessness in her mind. For many years, she had lived in this bungalow not merely as a housekeeper, but as if she were the mistress of the house itself. Now over fifty-five years of age, she was a tall, slender woman. Her sharp nose, deep-set eyes, and haughty demeanor suggested a certain darkness buried deep within her soul.

For years, she and her own daughter had lived a life of luxury within these walls. Now, she reflected with mounting bitterness on how the arrival of her master's daughter would strip her of her status and demote her once again to the mere rank of a housekeeper.

Driven by her inner arrogance and cold nature, she stood there secretly cursing the young Miss Anderson.

Just then, a horse-drawn carriage pulled up and stopped in front of the house. A young maidservant named Martha rushed toward the entrance. She had been waiting with breathless anticipation for the arrival of the noble young lady she had never met. All the servants gathered at the front of the bungalow, lining up with great discipline. Finally, Sarah Manson stepped forward, her hands folded behind her back in a composed manner.

As she stepped down from the carriage, eighteen-year-old Anne Mary Anderson looked around at her surroundings with curiosity. She turned toward the servants and offered a gentle smile. Everyone stood frozen, staring at Anne Mary in astonishment. Truly, she was a vision of beauty—but it was a different kind of beauty than they had expected. It wasn't just a delicate loveliness; she possessed a majestic, noble elegance. Her eyes reflected intelligence, kindness, and an unmistakable sense of observation.

There was a fearless quality in her gaze, an inner strength that was impossible to ignore.

Though Anne's majestic appearance momentarily shook Sarah Manson's resolve, the housekeeper quickly composed herself. She knew she had to establish her authority over this young girl immediately.

"Welcome... Miss Anne. We welcome you to the Anderson Bungalow. I am Sarah Manson, the head housekeeper who has managed this estate for many years."

"I am pleased to meet you, Mrs. Manson," Anne replied with her characteristic gentle smile. She then turned her attention toward the other servants. "And who are all of you...?"

Before they could answer, Sarah Manson cut in.

"They are just the lowly servants here. Please, Miss, you should come inside."

Understanding the head housekeeper's arrogance, Anne let out a little smile.

"To me, you all look exactly the same... so, I would like to get to know everyone."

As Sarah Manson turned red with suppressed rage, Anne went to each and every person, shaking their hands and introducing herself. This simple act immediately sparked a deep sense of affection for Anne among all the servants. However, from the very moment she stepped inside the house, a slight sense of anxiety settled in Anne's mind. Though she and her father had never shared a particularly close bond, she realized that the life she had led in India and the life she was destined to lead here were as different as the earth and the sky.

From that first encounter, Anne felt no great fondness for Sarah Manson and the feeling was entirely mutual. Sarah sensed that Anne was a formidable individual; yet, even as this thought crossed her mind, she could not have imagined what might happen in the future.

Sarah and her daughter, Lily, later joined Anne for the afternoon meal.

Lily was a character entirely different from her mother. Anne perceived her as being genuinely simple-hearted and modest. Despite her mother's nature, Lily was a gentle girl. At the dining table, she would steal shy glances at Anne and smile, yet she remained quiet, never uttering a word.

"To tell the truth, Miss Anne... I only saw you once before. That was when you were a very little girl. At that time, your mother was still among the living," Sarah Manson said, her voice trailing off into a heavy silence.

"Ah... and why, Miss Anne, have you not even touched this roasted mutton? You haven't even looked at it."

"It isn't for any specific reason... I simply do not have a heart cold enough to kill animals who breathe the same air and live on this earth just as we do. To taste the flesh of a creature that died in pain... that would only bring pain to my own heart!" Anne replied.

Sarah Manson looked at her with immense surprise.

"I have never encountered anyone who thinks quite like that. So, Miss Anne, you are a follower of non-violence then?" There was a trace of sarcasm in Sarah's tone.

"In that case, Miss Anne, you should not come to England. If people here hear you speak such things, they will surely think you've gone mad..."

"Mrs. Manson... what people think does not hinder my principles. People look at others from the range of their own thoughts. For those who look at the world from a narrow perspective, those who see the world broadly will always appear strange."Sarah Manson fell silent.

Anne was a very different kind of young woman. She looked at the world through a unique lens; her heart was filled with a deep love for the entire world. She never harbored a thought of hurting anyone. To her, the distinctions between poor and rich, or class and status, were non-existent. It was this very nature that had created a great distance between her and her father. Indeed, it was this disconnect that had ultimately led to her being sent away to England.

Chapter 2

The view from the window

After the afternoon meal, Martha escorted Anne to her room. It was located on the second floor, at the far-left corner. After passing several rooms and walking to the very end of the corridor, they reached the largest room, which had been prepared for Anne. However, it was clear that she had been intentionally placed far apart from the rest of the household.

"This is the largest and most luxurious room in the house, Miss Anne..." Martha said with a friendly smile. "In the past, the elders of the Anderson family used to give this room to their favorite child. But for at least forty years, no one has stayed in here..."

"Really...?" Anne asked as she stepped into the room.

The vast space was remarkably neat and clean. Despite the years, the heavy wooden furniture remained sturdy and elegant.

"You must have worked very hard, Martha, to get this place so orderly. Regardless of the past, I feel I shall like this room very much!"

"I am so glad to hear that, Miss Anne! Now, please take some rest. I have placed all your clothes and belongings in the wardrobe. If you need me at any time, just pull that bell cord over there..."

"Pull the cord! I will be here in a minute."

"Thank you very much. I would hate to trouble you unless it is absolutely necessary," Anne replied with her characteristic humility. With a smile, Martha left the room.

Though the journey had been long and exhausting, Anne had no intention of sleeping. She had no idea how long she was meant to stay here. All she wanted was change. Yet, she felt that the changes occurring were not necessarily for the best. Truthfully, she had never agreed with the decisions or ideas of her father, the Governor. For that reason, there was no warm bond between them.

With a sigh, Anne let her eyes wander around the room. She was instantly drawn to the ancient paintings hanging there. She loved everything she saw. For someone who had spent eighteen years in India, this was a starkly different world.

Even more than the room itself, Anne was enchanted by everything it contained. Moving with slow, quiet steps, she walked over to the desk beside the window.

The view she saw through the glass drew a sudden breath from her. She finally had the chance to see the small village nestled among the mountain ridges that she had noticed from afar. She smiled to herself. A sense of lightness settled over her mind, and her eyes drifted toward a small hill situated very close to the house.

On top of that hill stood a massive oak tree. It was clearly many years old. As she looked closer, she noticed something amidst the bushes and flowers surrounding the base of the tree. There were small stone structures.

"A tomb...? In such a place?" she whispered in astonishment. "High up on a mountain peak... in such a lonely spot? Why would anyone bury a human being there? You can't even get up there easily!"

Anne continued to stare at it, her mind filled with a profound sense of wonder. The sight of that grave in such a lonely place managed to stir her heart deeply. Because of the beauty of nature surrounding it, the fear she had felt moments ago vanished into thin air.

"Good morning, Miss Anne!" Martha said in a cheerful voice. "You are up very early."

"Good morning, Martha! I suppose I've just gotten used to it."

"Miss Anne... you are the one who should be giving orders in this house now, not Mrs. Manson. We are all waiting to serve you with great happiness!"

"Oh! Is that so? Then, Martha... what is that I see up on the small hill? Is it a tomb?"

Martha's face instantly changed. She looked at Anne with surprise.

"A tomb? What tomb, Miss Anne? On which small hill?"

"The one visible from my window..."

Martha looked out the window and let out a startled sound. "Truly, Miss Anne... I only just noticed it today. I've been here for three years, but I've never seen that place before. I think the row of large trees in the garden usually blocks our view from below. If this sight troubles you..."

"No, no, Martha. I actually like this room," Anne said.

Chapter 3

The sorrow of the gardener

After breakfast that morning, Anne walked through the garden to observe her surroundings. It was a very lonely area. There was nothing much to do inside the house, so Anne spent her time wandering idly.

Most of her time after that was spent with the gardener, Andrew. He was about sixty years old and was a man of constant sorrow, never seen to be happy. He treated Sarah Manson with a sense of distance. Having served at the Anderson mansion for many years, Anne enjoyed hearing from him the stories of her father's childhood.

"Have you not grown tired of working as a gardener here for so long, Andrew?" Anne asked one day as he was cleaning the greenhouse.

"One gets tired, but for some things, we must have patience..."

Anne looked at Andrew for a moment. Her mind sensed that this man possessed a good character, but he was suffering from a pain that could not be easily removed.

"You don't like Mrs. Manson very much... is that so, Andrew?"

"I hate her, Miss Anne... I hate her...!" he growled with sudden anger. Anne took a step back. "If your father hadn't forbidden me from staying here as a gardener, she would have driven me out long ago. That wicked woman...!"

"Has she done something so wrong to you that it creates such a great hatred?" Anne asked in surprise.

"She destroyed my life... if she hadn't been here, by now..." He suddenly fell silent.

"Miss Anne... you remind me of so many old things! I felt from the very first day I saw you that you are a good person. That is why I feel fear about you!"

Anne felt a slight unease. Was Andrew mentally ill? Or was he suffering because of some past event? She looked into his eyes and saw a pain unlike any she had seen in a man's eyes before. She approached him like a daughter approaching a father and placed her hand gently on his shoulder.

"Andrew, what happened...?"

The elderly man's voice trembled with deep resentment, and while he did not try to explain further, he remained looking at Anne.

"Miss Anne... look at the sky. It is gathering dark clouds... run home quickly now, or you will get soaked..."

Chapter 4

The girl in the mist

Anne sighed and began walking toward the house. Her eyes turned toward the small hill where the grave was located. Because of the dense trees surrounding the house, it was difficult to see clearly. Her mind began to fill with restless feelings. Once inside her room, she sat by the desk and prepared to write a letter to her father. However, Andrew's behavior kept coming back to her mind.

She realized Andrew was suffering from a secret pain. Even through Sarah Manson's arrogance, Anne caught glimpses of something dark. As she started to write, the first drops of rain began to fall. A cold wind blew over her, making her shiver. She quickly leaned toward the window to close it, and that was when she saw it.

She stood frozen. For a long time, she remained motionless, staring out. Her eyes were fixed on the small hill where the tomb lay. There, she saw someone standing, looking back at her with surprise.

It was a girl, perhaps fifteen or sixteen years old. Her hair was messy, blowing in the wind. She was holding a bouquet of white flowers. As she stood there looking at Anne, the wind whipped the rain across her face. Suddenly, realizing that Anne was watching her, the girl became startled. She quickly ran down the slope behind the oak tree.

Anne remained frozen. She ran to her bed and sat down, her heart racing. "My God, who was that girl...? Why did I get so flustered seeing her? What... who is she? A ghost?"

"Do I know her? I remember... I remember well... or do I? No, I don't remember... does that mean she isn't someone who belongs to that tomb? My God... is she a ghost? Oh God, am I going crazy? Would a ghost bring flowers to their own grave...? If only there were someone here I could talk to..."

That night at the dinner table, Anne remained quite silent. She tried her best to avoid Sarah Manson. Lily sat quietly as always, never bothering anyone and eating her meal with polite manners. Since the day she arrived, not more than a few words had been exchanged between Lily and Anne. During the meal, Sarah Manson noticed Anne's distant mood and her temper began to rise.

"Well, Miss Anne... what I tell you is for your own good as a daughter of a noble family. It is better not to associate too much with the servants... it doesn't suit your status."

""Mrs. Manson... what exactly are you trying to say?"

"It is about Andrew, my dear young lady. He was a man who had become half-mad."

"Oh! Is that so?" Anne inquired. "Even so, Mrs. Manson, I never sensed that. To me, it felt as though he was someone enduring a great deal of pain—as if someone, or something, had robbed him of something precious."

Sarah Manson looked at Anne with wide, startled eyes. The young woman continued her meal in silence for a moment, yet Anne noticed from the corner of her eye that Sarah's hands were trembling.

"Very well, young lady. Then listen closely... Your father sent you here because of the great trust he placed in me. I have served this family for generations. That is why I am telling you: it will be easier for you to live in this mansion if you listen to what I say!"

Suddenly, everything fell into a heavy silence. After serving the tea, Martha hurriedly left the room. There was a sharp, threatening edge to Sarah Manson's voice. Sensing this, Lily—now pale as a white lily—looked toward her mother, as if to show she had no connection to this conversation and no desire to be part of it.

Yet, for a moment, a stubborn defiance flickered in Anne's eyes. She looked back at Sarah Manson with a cold, steady gaze.

"...Oh! So that's how it is, Mrs. Manson? In that case, you must have grown weary of this job after all these years. Now the time has come for you to take your rest. I shall write to Father immediately. I will tell him that we need a new housekeeper."

Until Anne rose from the dining table and departed, Sarah Manson remained with her head bowed, her eyes fixed downward. Her heart was deeply shaken. Sarah realized that Anne was not a young woman who could be easily suppressed or intimidated; her first threat against Sarah's expectations had been met with a sharp, decisive blow.

In truth, that night, as she went to her room, Anne added to the letter she had already begun writing to her father. She wrote that because of Sarah Manson's sharp tongue and behavior, Sarah should leave the house at once. However, Anne knew that it would take at least a month for this letter to reach her father's hands.With a heavy sigh, Anne curled herself up on her bed.

Chapter 5

Meeting the *'Cursed Girl'*

Anne woke suddenly. Whether it was because of the biting chill that filled the room or some other reason, she could not tell. It was far too early to be awake. Unable to endure the cold air, she get out of bed. As a faint, pale light filtered into the room, Anne drew back the curtains. Outside, the garden was draped in a thick mist.

It was then that Anne saw her—the same girl she had seen the previous day, standing near the tomb at the small hill. Because of the frost gathered on the window glass, Anne was certain the girl could not see her. Narrowing her eyes, Anne watched her intently. The girl stood as she had before, her head and half of face covered with a scarf, likely to shield herself from the harsh cold. She sat at the foot of the huge Oak tree, staring toward the grave.

Suddenly, a bold idea entered Anne's mind. Removing her nightclothes, she quickly dressed in a gown and a thick coat. Wrapping a scarf around her neck, she prepared to head outside.

She looked through the window once more at the girl beneath the Oak tree. The girl remained there, motionless. Without wasting a moment, Anne hurried toward the main entrance.

The door was locked. The entire household was still deep in sleep. Anne let herself out through a side door and stepped into the garden. The atmosphere was filled with a ghostly, pale light. She moved toward the small hill, her footsteps hurried and anxious. A moment later, she reached the small hill. Behind a thicket of laurel bushes, she saw the girl, still lost in thought.

Anne realized that her approach had gone unnoticed. The girl's back was turned toward her. To gain the stranger's attention, Anne called out to her loudly.

The startled girl stood up abruptly. When she saw the noble-looking young woman standing before her, she was seized by a great fear and tried to hide behind the oak tree.

"Oh God... my lady!" the words escaped the girl's lips involuntarily.

"You... you know me?" Anne asked, her voice tinged with surprise.

"Oh, please, I beg of you, don't stay here. Why have you come here like this? I came here because I saw you..."

"My lady... please, go away from here. Don't try to talk to me. No one talks to me. Because I am a cursed thing!"

"Cursed? By what?" Anne shouted back. "I came through this shivering cold just to see you and speak with you. What do you mean by 'a cursed thing'?"

"That is what people call me..." the girl whispered, no longer trying to hide her face. "I don't want anything bad to happen to you because of me. Please, leave this place!"

"Oh... is that so? And what is your name?" Anne asked.

"Helly..."

"That is a very beautiful name. Helly, nothing good has happened in my life for a long time. Nothing bad is going to happen just because I saw you. So please... come and talk to me."

After a moment, the girl stepped away from the Oak tree. She stood before Anne, looking timid and fearful. In truth, she was not an ordinary sight to behold.

Helly was a girl of remarkable beauty, her skin as white as a lily. Though her large blue eyes held a fearful and innocent expression, she was different—not because of her features, but because her half of face was almost entirely covered by the scars of a terrible, old burn! The beautiful girl had been left with a distorted appearance by this cruel injury. Her clothes were old and tattered, giving her a disheveled look.

Yet, Anne did not seem disturbed by her appearance. Seeing that Anne showed no sign of disgust or fear, Helly seemed struck with wonder.

"Wait! Helly, I feel as though we have met somewhere before... but I cannot remember where," Anne said in a steady voice.

"My lady, I was waiting for you... but I did not know you were coming here to this house…again.." Helly replied in a low tone.

"Why do you come here? Is that grave for someone in your family?" Anne asked.

Helly looked away, her eyes clouded with a constant, lingering pain.

"It is not for someone of my family, my lady... This person who was lost to this world was my only friend. Even speaking of it brings me such agony...".

"Oh, please forgive me," Anne said softly. "I am Anne Marry Anderson. You know of me, don't you?".

"Who does not know of my lady? But meeting me will only bring you misfortune," elly replied.

"Why do you say such a thing?" Anne asked.

"Because that is what everyone says," Helly murmured.

"But I do not think so," Anne countered. "I must go now, Helly, but we shall meet again. I spend my time here in such loneliness, You are the first person I have truly met in this village. Where do you live?".

"I live quite far from here, my lady. Every day, when the sun begins to set, I come here. But today, I came early in the morning... Now I must go. I come here every single day...".

Though she knew she had to return before the servants of the house awoke, Anne wished to stay a moment longer.

"Well, I have a little more time. They will think that I am still asleep," Anne said with a small smile.

"You are very strange, Helly. I feel as though you are trying to hide from this world," Anne observed.

"Yes, little lady. I have no one. No one comes for me. Everyone says I am a cursed girl. Because I am deformed, the people of the village do not even wish to look at me. They say I brought bad luck to my family... and that I am a burden," Helly said, her voice heavy with sorrow.

"That is why I come here in secret, where people cannot see me," she added.

"But I do not see it that way at all," Anne said firmly. "You do not look like someone who brings misfortune to anyone. Why do they say these things? Are the people here truly that cruel?".

"My lady... on the day I was born, my house caught fire. My parents were trapped in the flames and perished. My brother, who was just a young child himself, jumped into the fire and saved my life. But this face... this deformity... this bad luck has followed me my whole life. He was the one who saved me, and yet who cares me," Helly said with deep grief.

"My brother looked after me. But I do not go where he is, for fear that people will look down on him because of me," she whispered.

Anne felt a sharp pang of sympathy. She wished she could reach out and comfort this girl whose face told such a tragic story.

"Very well. But it is wrong to say you are cursed. I am glad I met you. I will come again, Helly. Goodbye for now! Let us meet here again tomorrow morning," Anne said.

With a kind parting word, Anne turned and walked quickly back toward the house.

Chapter 6

Superstitions and Shadows

Anne felt a profound sense of sadness for the girl. How could an innocent girl, orphaned and left helpless, be cast out by an entire village? She could not understand it. Helly's beautiful blue eyes, filled with such sorrow and emptiness, haunted her thoughts. It was for this reason that Anne's own face was now clouded with a heavy gloom. She watched as Helly disappeared among the trees. Andrew has started his work so early in the morning and he looked at Anne with surprise.

"Little lady!! Why have you woken up so early...? My God, you look as though you've been crying...?".

"Ah? No... no, Andrew. I just felt like taking a walk early this morning!" Anne replied, her voice filled with surprise.

Andrew looked at Anne with profound astonishment before turning his gaze back to the path she had just traveled.

"Alone??" he asked, his voice thick with concern. "I don't think today is quite the right kind of day for a walk like that..."

"Yes... but I just felt like I had to get out," Anne replied quietly. She thought to herself that she needed to talk to him for a while, if only to ease the weight pressing on her heart. "Andrew, you're up so early. Are you starting work already?"

"Yes, little lady," he replied. He was still looking at the young girl, his eyes wide with that same lingering surprise. "I'm the first one to wake in this bungalow. Why? Because I find it so incredibly difficult to get through every night here..." He trailed off, his final words barely more than a haunting murmur.

"Oh! Is that so?" Anne asked, still troubled by the strangeness she saw in the old man's face. "Andrew, what exactly does it mean to be 'cursed'?"

The question hit him like a physical blow. Andrew's expression shifted, looking like a man suffering from a sudden nervous affliction. His mouth hung slightly agape as he stared at Anne, unmoving.

"I asked... what did you mean by those words, Andrew?" Anne pressed, her voice dropping to a low, serious tone.

"Little lady! What are you asking me? That... that... I don't know, truly..." He began to stammer, his composure crumbling. "But some simple people think... that when many troubles befall helpless people, they are just... unfortunate."

"But this is the nineteenth century! In England!" Anne countered firmly. "Are there still people who believe in such foolish superstitions? I can't even imagine it."

"But, little lady... why did you ask me such a thing?" Andrew asked, his voice trembling.

"It's nothing. I shouldn't think about it too much. I'm going now, Andrew. Have a good day!"

As she walked away, Anne felt certain that Andrew was suffering from some form of mental distress. She bit her lower lip, noticing the other servants watching her from the kitchen with bewildered expressions. Ignoring them, she retreated to her room and closed the door firmly behind her.

"It's a beautifully sunny day today, Helly!" Ann said, looking at the girl sitting at the foot of the oak tree. She offered a gentle smile. Thinking that climbing near to oak tree might be dangerous for her, Anne sat down on a stone ledge distant from Oak tree and tomb .

"To be honest, Helly, I don't think it was a good idea for me to come here, after all I've thought about it."

"Why do you think that, my lady?"

"Everything here happens in such a strange way... I feel a dark, gloomy shadow hanging over everything."

"I feel the same, my lady. I am so lonely... it's a pain I can hardly bear. But when I met you, I felt a joy I haven't known in years."

"I feel the same, Helly. I was tired of having no one to talk to. If only that woman, Sarah Manson, wasn't managing this house—how much better would it be?"

"Stay away from her," Helly warned urgently.

Anne looked at the white flowers in Helly's lap with surprise. Helly had never expressed anything but pain before, yet now she spoke with a sharp edge.

"From whom?"

"From Sarah." Helly's voice was cold.

"Why do you say that? Do you know Mrs. Manson?"

Helly simply nodded her head up and down.

"She is a devil!" Helly burst out with sudden, sharp anger.

Anne stared at her, stunned. Was this what Andrew had been trying to tell her?

"Why do you say that, Helly? What wrong has she done to you?"

Helly bit her lip and looked down at the ground. Her face darkened with a fierce, smoldering rage. The sight of it sent a chill through Anne.

"My lady... Please go now."

"But—" Anne started to speak, but the sound of footsteps crunching through the thicket.

Suddenly, the elderly Andrew appeared before them. Anne, startled, immediately turned her gaze toward the little mountain peak. It was a stroke of luck—Helly had already vanished. But as Anne followed Andrew toward the house, she felt him watching her with a sharp, piercing look that felt like a warning.

"Little Lady... have you come for a walk today as well? Alone?"

"I heard the sound of someone talking to themselves from a distance, and that's what brought me this way," Old man said, turning toward Anne.

"Yes... it was me," Anne replied softly. "I've loved talking to the trees and the bushes ever since I was a little girl. I still do it."

Andrew seemed lost in a different world. He stood there, calm and silent, gazing toward the hill and the thicket of trees.

"Well then, let's go, Little Lady. It's already lunchtime."

As they made their way back toward the Anderson Bungalow, Sarah Manson watched them from an upper-floor window. Anne caught a glimpse of her; Sarah's eyes were fixed on them with a look of pure coldness and resentment. Startled by the intensity of that gaze, Sarah Manson quickly stepped away from the window and vanished into the shadows of the room.

"I wrote to Father and told him that we need a new housekeeper now," Anne said, turning to Andrew. "Lately,

Sarah Manson is always following me around... she's constantly watching me."

The older man looked at her gravely. "Little Lady, do you think Mr. Anderson will ever ask Sarah to leave? Do you think he'd ever send her away?"

"I know that Father and I don't always agree on things," Anne admitted. "But he loves me dearly. I believe he would do anything I asked of him."Andrew sighed, his expression filled with a quiet pity. "Even so... John Anderson will never cast that woman out of this house. That is a certainty."

Anne looked at him, stunned by the conviction in his voice.

Chapter 7

The Warning

As time trickled by, Anne began to settle into the rhythms of the Anderson Bungalow. Among the staff, she became a well-loved figure, known for her pleasant nature. However, Sarah Manson lived in a state of perpetual agitation. She watched as the life she had built over the years began to crumble with the arrival of this young girl. Driven by bitterness, Sarah spent her nights weaving dark schemes to reclaim her lost influence.

Despite the tension in the house, Anne found moments of peace. Every three or four days, she would wander down to the small hill to meet Helly. As usual, Helly was sitting at the base of large Oak tree, looking weary and frail. It was clear to Anne that she seemed different from the other children.

Helly's face, usually pale, would light up with a joyful smile whenever she saw Anne approaching. She listened to her with genuine care. Yet, Helly never truly answered her questions or spoke about the details of her own life. To the world, she remained an enigma—a secret she held close to her heart.

After two months of silence, a letter finally arrived from Anne's father. But instead of bringing her peace, the contents left her feeling deeply unsettled.

In his letter, her father stated firmly that she would not consider any housekeeper other than Sarah Manson. Furthermore, he revealed that he had resigned from all his official positions and intended to move to England to live out his days in quiet retirement. He explained that since Anne was no longer there, he saw no reason to stay.

Anne let out a heavy sigh. Were the Andrew's warnings coming true?

"How could Father make such a decision? He doesn't know what Mrs Manson is really like," Anne whispered to herself. "She makes me feel like she could cast me out of here at any moment."

Just then, a sharp knock sounded at her door.

"Come in... the door is open," Anne called out, her heart racing.

Martha entered the room, her eyes swollen and red from crying. She looked at Anne with a gaze full of sorrow.

"My lady Anne... I've come to say goodbye to you," she whispered, her voice trembling.

"What? Goodbye?" Anne’s voice rose in shock and confusion.

At that moment, tears began to stream down Martha's face. She looked down at the floor, unable to meet Anne's eyes. "Mrs Manson... she told me I must leave this house immediately. But my lady, I swear I have done nothing wrong. I haven't made a single mistake, I swear you!".

"How can she do such a thing?" Anne asked, her anger flaring. "You are my maid! How can Mrs Manson do something like this without even asking me?".

"Oh, My lady... please, don't let there be trouble between the two of you because of me," Martha pleaded, but she could say no more. Anne, her face set in determination, turned and marched out of the room with quick, firm strides.

Sarah Manson was in the drawing room, reclining in a comfortable chair and focused on her knitting. Even when Anne burst into the room, Sarah didn't look up, continuing her work with a cold, detached calmness.

"Sarah Manson! I want to know why you are sending Martha away!" Anne demanded.

Sarah set her knitting aside and stood up slowly, her expression unreadable. "I am the one who hired Martha for service, Little Miss. I have the authority to act as I see fit in this house. You would do well to follow my lead".

"Mrs Manson, I have been very patient with your arrogance," Anne countered, her voice shaking with indignation. "Martha is not going anywhere. She is more than just a servant to me—she is my friend!".

"My father will come soon here, He expects many things to change when he arrives. There will be retirement party for you in this house, Mrs Manson—you can be sure of that!".

Sarah Manson let out a short, mocking laugh. "That will never happen, Little Miss. Mr. Anderson knows exactly how loyal I have been to this family".

"That may be, but you clearly don't understand how much a father loves his daughter," Anne replied firmly. "He would do anything in this world for me".

At those words, Sarah Manson momentarily faltered, a flicker of uncertainty crossing her face as she realized the truth in Anne's statement. Without a word, Sarah turned and walked away, her face dark with silent resentment. But even as she left, a new, hidden plan began to form in the depths of her mind.

Chapter 8

Justice in the flames

The evening was fading. Anne sat at her desk, jotting down notes, when she suddenly noticed a figure. It was Helly, standing near the Oak tree on small hill, signaling her to come closer. Helly wore a look of pleasantness that Ann had never seen before—a strange, newfound light in her eyes.

"So, Helly... how are you?" Anne asked, looking at the girl sitting at the foot of the Oak tree. Seeing the peaceful expression on Helly's face, as soft as a white flower, brought a sense of relief to Anne.

"I'm well,my lady... very well."

"You seem happy today...?"

"Yes, my lady... I am going to be free of everything. I am going to find peace... that is why I wanted to see you one last time..."

Anne watched her friend in silence. The strange words Helly spoke make her confused. Anne knew from experience that probing her with questions would be useless. Regardless, Helly had been the first true friend to enter Anne's life.

"My lady... you were so kind to me always… this Oak tree remain silent because it knows too many secrets" Helly whispered softly.

"Even so, there were things I hoped for... things I could never do. Helly... do you know? My father is coming here in another six months. Then, I will take you with me to Anderson Mansion. Because then, I'll only have to listen to what my father says... I will send Sarah Manson away from here somehow... You are my best friend. I want the whole village to know that. After that, no one will call you a 'cursed girl' anymore... In the spring, we can go to the forest together to pick flowers... we can ride horses around the village..."

As Anne spoke, Helly remained quiet, a tear overflowing from her eye. The faint smile lingering on her lips suggested she was lost in a distant memory.

"My lady... it's time to say good bye. Go carefully... be especially wary of Sarah Manson. Be safe... no matter what happens, I am here for you! Goodnight...!"

"Goodnight, Helly!" Anne replied, her heart heavy with her friend's cryptic words as she walked back toward Anderson Mansion.

That night, dinner was a silent, tense affair. Sarah Manson did not speak a word to them.

Later, as Anne headed to her room to sleep, the night was already deep. Upon entering her chamber, her eyes widened in surprise; a letter lay upon her bed. She quickly picked it up and began to read.

Dear Miss Anne,

I feel I should have told you this before. There is something important I must tell you regarding Sarah Manson. If you can, come to the grain storehouse at 11 p.m. Do not let anyone see you.

From your faithful servant, Andrew.

Anne placed the letter on her bedside table and exhaled a long sigh. 'What on earth is happening here?' "Strange things... anyway, Andrew... maybe he can tell me why he hates Sarah Manson..." Anne quickly wrapped a shawl around herself.

'But how did Andrew get this letter onto my bed? Perhaps Martha sent it through someone...?'

She began to think about the location of the grain storehouse. It was situated a short distance from the mansion. Anne had never gone there, day or night. She only knew it had been abandoned for years. Nevertheless, lighting a candle, Ann began to descend the stairs. Fortunately, everyone had retired to their rooms; she heard only the sound of someone washing dishes in the kitchen. Anne slipped through a side window and stepped into the dark night.

The night was warm. The surroundings were shrouded in a thick, pitch-black gloom. Anne walked cautiously toward the storehouse. As she drew near, she saw the faint glow of a candle flickering inside. She had covered nearly two hundred yards by then.

Reaching the storehouse, she saw the door was slightly opened. A sliver of candlelight spilled out into the darkness.

"Andrew... are you there?" Anne stepped slowly into the building.

Suddenly, a heavy blow struck the back of her head. Anne collapsed to the floor! As she drifted in and out of consciousness, she heard a woman's sharp, piercing laugh. She struggled to open her eyes. Standing before her, holding a heavy club, was Sarah Manson.

"You must be so happy to hear from Andrew! Now you can learn all about Sarah Manson... Your little life is over, Anne Mary Anderson...! Your game ended today... this is the end of the Anderson family...!" Sarah Manson laughed like a predator that had finally cornered its prey.

It was a laugh fueled by pure, unadulterated hatred. Anne tried to move, but her body refused to obey. She lost consciousness again.

When Anne finally came to, she felt a throbbing, violent headache. Simultaneously, she felt a suffocating heat. She looked around—the grain storehouse was engulfed in roaring flames! Someone had set the building on fire while she lay trapped inside. To the semi-conscious Anne, everything felt like a nightmare.

A moment later, she found herself lying on the grass in the dark night. She was breathing with great difficulty. A few yards away, the storehouse was being swallowed by the rising fire.

She looked at the face of the young woman leaning over her. Though half the face was scarred, there was a triumphant smile of peace and victory upon it.

"My lady... I saved you! I was able to save your life..."

"Helly!" Anne whispered with great difficulty.

"Yes...my lady... Now I can go... I have found my peace... justice has been served," Helly murmured softly.

Simultaneously, the agonizing cry of a woman and the sound of several people's footsteps reached Anne's ears. Just as she turned her gaze toward Helly's eyes, which were shining like stars, she slipped back into unconsciousness.

When she finally opened her eyes, Ann saw only the white ceiling of her luxurious room. As she wondered if what she had experienced earlier was merely a terrible dream, her head began to throb. Reaching up to her forehead, she felt bandages wrapped around her head.

She quickly looked around the room. Standing beside her bed was Martha.

"Thank the Heavens! My lady, you've regained consciousness...!" Martha exclaimed, and at her shout, several other servants and Andrew rushed into the room.

As Anne struggled to sit up on the bed, their faces, heavy with sorrow, turned toward her.

"Oh, Lord... Little lady... I lived in fear every day that this would happen... and in the end, it all came to pass exactly as I feared. But this time, goodness has triumphed," Andrew said, gently stroking her head with fatherly affection.

"We all woke up because of a woman's scream..." Martha began to explain.

"When we woke up, someone was shouting that the grain storehouse was on fire. By the time we ran there, the flames were leaping high into the sky. No one could get close enough to control it. When we reached the source of those screams, we saw a woman rolling on the ground, engulfed in flames and wailing in agony...!"

"That was Sarah Manson...! We managed to extinguish the fire on her body... but my lady, it was a mercy that you did not have to witness that sight. She was hideously burned, wounded, and disfigured. In the midst of her final breaths, she cried out in pain and rage, 'Why was that cursed oil bottle poured all over my body?'"

Anne looked at the group in stunned silence. If that were the case, Sarah Manson—the woman who had tried to kill her—had killed herself by mistake.

Andrew sighed and looked at Anne.

"Little lady, Sarah meant to strike you down and then burn you in the grain storehouse. But by some fluke of fate, the fire she intended for you caught her own body instead. The oil spilled on her. When the warehouse ignited, she was caught in the blaze. We understood everything once we read the letter left on your table. Little lady... I know you went there because you trusted me... but what none of us can understand is how you managed to escape such a brutal attack and make it out alive."

"That's true, my lady..." Martha added.

"My lady, you were lying on the grass several yards away from the burning storehouse."

Anne looked at them with a look of pure bewilderment.

"Why didn't you see Helly? My friend! She was the one who saved me...!"

"Helly...? Who is that?" the servants whispered among themselves in confusion.

But Andrew, his eyes wide with shock, stared at Anne.

"My lady... who did you say it was?"

"Helly... she is my friend! She saved my life, Andrew... she was the one who pulled me out of the fire. I went to the small hill to meet her. We are friends...!"

Andrew let out a deep, inexplicable sigh. After a long silence, he spoke again.

"Yes, Little lady... now I understand. You were Helly's friend! That is why Helly came to save you...!"

"Does that mean you know Helly, Andrew...?"

"Yes, Little lady... I have so much to tell you. But before anything else, you must rest..."

"What I don't understand is why Sarah Manson hated me so much..." Anne said, following Andrew out of the house into the yard.

"There is a great reason for that, Little lady. But before all of that, there is a place we must go..."

"Truly, I feel very sad about Helly, Andrew. Five days have passed since this incident. But since then, I haven't seen her again. I couldn't even thank her. I am alive today because of her... I am indebted to her for my entire life, Andrew..."

"Yes, that is true, Little lady. But Helly will never come again."

"Andrew... why do you say like that? Helly will come tomorrow or the day after..."

"No, Little lady. Let me explain everything to you. Come with me to the tomb beneath the Oak tree on the small hill. Everything starts from there... just like your friendship with Helly began there."

Anne followed Andrew with a look of wonder on her face. Eventually, they saw the tomb beneath the Oak tree, surrounded by overgrown bushes and wild flowers. Looking at this burial ground, where every secret seemed bound, Anne felt a profound sense of unease. She thought about the many times she had sat with Helly on the small Hill and talked. However, for the first time, Anne climbed to the top of that hill with Andrew's help. As she leaned toward a tombstone hidden among the wild bushes, Andrew sat at the foot of the Oak tree. Anne's eyes widened as she read the inscription.

Isabella Anderson

A.D. 1800 - 1819

'We will hold you in our memory forever.'

Helly and Andrew

Anne turned to Andrew in utter shock.

"I don't understand any of this, Andrew... I don't understand anything... This person is from our lineage... But she died in the year 1819. That was thirty-seven years ago! But Helly! She said this was her friend's grave... but thirty-seven years ago...?"

"Little lady...Please sit here without getting agitated..." Andrew spoke in a calm, steady voice.

"Yes... everything happened thirty-seven years ago..."

Anne sat beside him at the foot of the Oak tree.

"I feel like there is a massive problem here, Andrew. Tell me everything... Who is Isabella? Then, who are Sarah Manson... Helly... and you? How are all these people connected to each other like links in a chain?"

"It is a very long story, Little lady. A very long story... but in the end, I am going to tell you all of it..." Andrew's dark, sorrowful eyes turned toward the blue, troubled sky. He wondered if that same sky had appeared this way decades ago. But who was with him under that sky on that day...?

****

37 Years Ago...

It was a brilliant day, the sun shining in all its glory. Andrew, a young man of twenty-seven, wiped the beads of sweat from his forehead as he walked toward his small cottage. His mind was occupied with thoughts of Isabella, the daughter of his employers, who had arrived at her parents' estate that very morning. Andrew worked as a driver at the Anderson bungalow, a job he had taken to earn enough money for his delayed higher education.

Richard Anderson and his wife had moved to the bungalow several years prior, but their only daughter, **Isabella**, had just arrived that morning to live with them after completing her studies.

As Andrew approached his home, he saw his sixteen-year-old sister, Helly, waiting for him impatiently. The moment he drew near, she ran toward him. Her eyes, which usually sparkled with youthful energy despite the scars that marred her face, were wide with excitement.

"Brother, did you see her? Did you see Andrew... I mean, the young mistress?" she asked breathlessly.

"Who?" Andrew teased, stepping inside the house. He placed a small parcel of sweets he had brought for her on a wooden bench. But Helly was too restless to care about the treats; she pushed the parcel aside.

"Did you see the young mistress, Isabella? What does she look like, Andrew?"

"Oh..." Andrew replied with a mischievous grin.

"Then you did see her! Did you actually see her? Tell me!"

"I didn't just see her," Andrew laughed. "She even shook my hand!"

"What? No!" Helly cried out. "Don't lie, Andrew... You are not that lucky!"

"Is that so? Well, if you don't believe me, go ask Old Tom!"

Helly sighed. "You know Old Tom never tells me anything clearly. Stop teasing and tell me about Miss Isabella."

"To put it simply," Andrew said, his expression softening, "she looks like a princess out of a fairy tale. She has the most beautiful, kind eyes, Helly. You won't believe it, but she is so humble. She shook hands with all of us servants before she even entered the mansion."

"That's why I said she touched my hand!" he added with a grin.

"Oh, Andrew... how lucky you are," Helly whispered, her voice tinged with longing. "I wish I could see her just once. Could you ever arrange for me to meet her?"

As she spoke, Helly caught a glimpse of her own reflection in a cracked piece of mirror. She looked at her scarred, distorted face and her hope withered. "No... never mind. If she sees me, she'll be frightened."

Andrew felt a pang of sorrow for his sister. He remembered that terrible day years ago—the day she was born. A fire had broken out in their home just as their parents took their final breaths. Andrew, only eleven at the time, had managed to pull his infant sister from the flames, but her face had already been severely burned.

Through a miracle of fate, Helly survived, but she grew up in a world that wasn't kind. While Andrew worked hard and pursued his education, Helly remained hidden. The villagers called her "the cursed girl," believing she brought ill fortune because her parents died the day she was born. Even their own grandmother had shared this belief. Ostracized by the village, she lived a confined life within the walls of their small hut.

Yet, Andrew loved her more than anything.

"Alright, Helly," Andrew said gently. "If you really want to see her, I have a plan."

Helly looked at her brother with renewed hope.

"The young mistress is staying in the room at the far end of the mansion—the one that belonged to the eldest child for generations. If you go to the large Oak tree on the hill this afternoon, you can see her through the open window."

"You're the best, Andrew!" Helly cheered.

That afternoon, Helly made her way to the hill. She hid behind the thick trunk of the old Oak tree, careful to keep her face partially obscured. Andrew had been right. Through the window, she saw a young woman leaning over a desk, writing intently. Helly watched in awe, struck by Isabella's grace.

"She is truly wonderful," Helly whispered to herself.

At that moment, Isabella looked up and glanced out the window. Her eyes met Helly's for a fleeting second. Startled, Helly quickly pulled back and hid behind the tree.

"Oh no, she saw me!" Helly gasped, covering her face with her hands. She didn't wait a second longer; she turned and ran back toward her cottage.

The next morning, Isabella was out walking, exploring the estate. She found herself near the large Oak tree where she had seen the girl the previous evening. Suddenly, she spotted Andrew walking toward her, carrying a small parcel. He handed it to a young girl standing by the tree and then hurried back toward the bungalow.

Isabella approached quietly. She found the girl sitting on the ground, leaning against the tree, greedily eating the sweets Andrew had brought.

When Helly sensed someone's presence and looked up, she froze in terror. For the first time, Isabella saw the girl's face clearly—the deep scars and the pain etched into her features.

"Oh...My lady... why... why did you come here?" Helly stammered, trembling as she tried to cover her face with her scarf.

"I saw you here yesterday also, so I wanted talk to you," Isabella said in a soft, calm voice. "Who are you? What is your name?"

"I'm Helly... but , please, My lady... it's unlucky for you to meet me. You shouldn't stay here. Please go..."

Isabella looked at her with a puzzled expression.

"What do you mean? Don't you want to be my friend? I thought people in the countryside were very friendly... perhaps I was wrong."

"It’s not like that,my lady... I am an unlucky girl. If I cross someone’s path, they say it brings them misfortune. That is what the people in this village believe."

Isabella smiled, her eyes narrowing slightly. "Blind superstition!"

"Why,my lady? Don’t you feel a sense of revulsion now that you know about me?" Helly asked, her voice trembling with fear.

"Revulsion...?" Isabella repeated, her voice filled with wonder. "We are all creations of Mother Nature. We are like the children of one mother. How could we ever feel revulsion toward another human being? Here, give me your hand and help me climb up this hill!"

Helly extended her hand toward Isabella.

Smiling sweetly, Isabella climbed to the top of the hill, rested her hands on her hips, and looked around at the surrounding landscape.

"How beautiful is this? Truly, how wonderful it is that I came here!" Isabella pointed toward a small cottage nestled in the distance. She turned to Helly and asked, "Is that where you live?"

"Yes, My lady..."

"I thought so... then Andrew...? He knows you, doesn't he? I saw our horse-carriage driver giving you a parcel of sweets earlier."

"That is my only brother... he is all I have in this world, my lady."

Isabella turned to Helly, her expression softening with kindness. "Then what about your mother and father...?"

With a heavy sigh, Helly laid bare her painful past.

"That was just an unfortunate event in your life, Helly... but because of it, you aren't someone who brings misfortune to others. That simply doesn't happen!" Isabella spoke with a firm, decisive voice.

"Do you know? Today, I was planning to take a stroll around the village with your brother. Andrew is indeed a good driver. But even so, to see the village properly, I need a good friend who knows the area well...!"

Helly looked at Isabella in pure amazement.

"It's settled then, Helly. You can do that for me, can't you? Be my guide for today?"

Helly's mouth hung open in shock. "My lady... what are you saying...?"

Before Helly could say another word, Isabella took her by the hand and began leading her down the hill. Soon, they reached the Anderson mansion. The servants standing in the courtyard watched them with wide-eyed wonder, wondering what disaster was about to unfold. Ignoring them, Isabella entered the mansion with her new 'guide.'

"Miss Isabella,... what is the meaning of this?" a maid asked, her voice hushed with fear.

"Oh, my God! What is this girl doing here? What a misfortune...!"

"No... there is no misfortune here. Look, from today, Helly will be my guide. She will help me find the most beautiful spots in this village. You will all realize that she isn't an unlucky person," Isabella said in a joyful tone.

"She doesn't bring bad luck to anyone...!"

In the midst of all this, Helly stood shivering. No one had ever spoken up for her like this before. No one had ever accepted her. She felt as though her entire life was about to change.

Hearing the loud conversation in the hall, Isabella's mother, Mrs. Anderson, walked calmly into the room. She was a very compassionate woman who knew nothing of the villagers' superstitions or their treatment of Helly.

"What is all this commotion? Isabella, I thought you had gone out... who is this?" Mrs. Anderson asked, looking at Helly with curious eyes.

"Mother... this is Helly, Andrew's sister. I thought she could help me see the beauty of the village today. But I need your permission, Mother," Isabella said with her usual cheerful charm.

Mrs. Anderson looked at the girl, who had been treated so unfairly by fate. She looked at her with a gaze full of motherly compassion. Mrs. Anderson understood her daughter's heart well; she knew Isabella never did anything without a good reason.

"That is a very good idea, child. That way, you won't feel lonely either," Mrs. Anderson said with a gentle smile.

The servants went about their duties with solemn expressions, each immersed in their respective tasks. Meanwhile, Isabella, radiating joy, walked toward the horse carriage alongside Helen. Andrew watched the two of them with a complex, unreadable gaze.

"Andrew, why do you look so worried? Your sister is coming with us today," Isabella said with a smile.

Andrew's eyes grew misty. He wondered how this noble young woman could treat his sister—a girl the entire village branded as "cursed"—with such profound kindness and sincerity.

Chapter 9

The best days ever

Truly, that day was the best day of Helly's life. They traveled forward through the narrow paths of the estate, passing lush green thickets. The villagers, who usually recognized the Anderson family carriage from a distance, were struck with utter astonishment when they peeked inside and saw Helly sitting there.

Though they were all curious, their amazement turned to bewilderment upon realizing the "cursed girl" was sitting right inside the carriage. Isabella, however, felt a deep sense of satisfaction. A naturally compassionate soul, she felt a strong protective instinct toward Helly. Until then, the entire village community had shunned Helly as an outcast; no one had ever looked at her with such warmth.

Indeed, Isabella's intention was to breathe new life into Helly's world. Because of the villagers' prejudice, Helly had spent her days hiding in the shadows of the estate, never walking with pride or confidence.

Now, the villagers watched them with great wonder. No one dared to say anything to Helly, nor did they have the courage to do so. They were intimidated by the presence of the noble daughter of the estate's powerful owner. Some looked at her with deep jealousy, wondering how a girl like Helly had managed to win the hearts of Anderson family.

Helly felt as though the day was passing with impossible speed. As they reached the grand gates of the Anderson mansion and the moment came to say goodbye, Isabella's face was lit with a joyful glow. Helly looked at Isabella for a long time with deep affection.

"My lady... I honestly don't know how I can ever repay the debt I owe you... to me... to me, all of this feels like a dream," Helly whispered.

"It is true, little lady. My sister was always the one being ignored by the world... but you gave her value today. We are both truly grateful to you," Andrew added with great happiness.

"Oh, it's nothing like that! Do you know how I feel? I feel like I found two very good friends today. I'm not a very social person myself, so I don't actually have many friends," Isabella replied modestly. "In the future, we will become even better friends. So, goodbye for today!"

With those words, Isabella turned and walked into the mansion.

With the onset of spring, the entire village was filled with the beauty of blooming flowers. There wasn't a place in the village where Isabella and Helly hadn't set foot. The young woman from London, now fully immersed in village life, found her best companion in Helly—the very girl the village had labeled as "cursed."

They would wander through the meadows, picking wild flowers together. While Helly helped decorate Isabella’s room with those flowers, Isabella was equally enthusiastic about decorating Helly's small cottage. On many bright mornings, the sight of these two—riding together on horseback was a rare and beautiful sight for the villagers.

Helly was often invited to the Anderson mansion for tea. She was treated not as the driver's sister, but as a dear friend of Miss Isabella.

However, Andrew had his reasons for being skeptical of them both. Deep down, Isabella had become Helly’s closest confidante. Previously, that place had belonged solely to Andrew. On the other hand, Helly had become Isabella’s friend and mentor. Even as the driver, Andrew was the one who usually held that position of trust. Yet, seeing their bond, he was more happy than anyone else.

Isabella also showed a talent for storytelling. Often, she would lie down under a tree and tell Helly fairy tales. Andrew, who usually took everything as a joke, would listen to the stories and occasionally interject with cynical questions.

"...And after that, the Prince and Princess lived happily ever after," Isabella concluded the story in a sweet voice.

"Does it really happen like that, Little lady?" Andrew asked with a smirk playing on his lips.

"I'm asking... why do stories always end with 'they lived happily ever after'? Does nothing bad ever happen in their lives after that? I'm asking because, at the very least, don't they face any sickness, epidemics, or even a simple toothache?"

Isabella's face turned a shade of rosy pink.

"Andrew... I think you are far too old for my stories! Go and read some scientific or literary book instead!"

"That's true, Andrew," Helly added, laughing. "You are much too old to be listening to our fairy tales!"

In the end, Andrew decided to keep his thoughts to himself. "It is not right for a mature, intelligent person like me to pay heed to such childish and foolish talk," he reasoned. Yet, until he reached the mansion, the echoes of their mocking laughter continued to ring in his ears. He tried to convince himself that everything was transpiring for the best—even better than he had anticipated.

It was truly a radiant morning. Andrew had only just finished cleaning the horse carriage when Isabella came running toward him, her face beaming with joy.

"Andrew... Andrew! I spoke about it... Father agreed!"

Andrew looked at the panting Isabella with a gaze he simply could not hide. "What is it, Little lady? What are you talking about?"

"Andrew, I'm not going to let you stay here without finishing your degree. I spoke with Father about it. He agreed to bear the expenses for you. Next month, you are going to London... to resume your studies!"

Andrew stared at her, helpless, his eyes wide with disbelief. To him, it felt too good to be true. "Little lady...! I..."

"You can't believe it, can you?" Isabella asked with a smile. "Helly was the one who told me. She said it was her wish for you to go to London and study. Then I talked with my father. That's why Father agreed to help you finish it now. Now, go home and tell Helly the good news!"

Chapter 10

The daughter of the shadow

Just then, a maid came running from the mansion in a state of great excitement. "Miss Isabella... Miss Isabella... please come to the mansion quickly. Mr. Manson has arrived...!"

"Alright... tell him I'm coming," Isabella replied, her face tightening slightly.

"Oh... the Master asked for Andrew to come along as well," the maid added before hurrying away.

"Even so, Andrew, I don't quite like Mr. Manson's arrival," Isabella confessed.

"Why do you say that, Little lady?"

"Perhaps he is here because of Mr. Manson has been trying to propose a marriage between his son, Godfrey Manson, and me. But it's not out of any honest intention. Mr. Manson knows that I will be the next heir to the Anderson fortune! That is why he wants me to marry his son. My mother and I realized this a long time ago. But Father still thinks of Mr.

Manson as his sincere school friend. The truth is quite different."

Andrew listened to Isabella's words in silence. However, he and all the other servants knew the situation well. The Manson family had once been a famous and wealthy clan, but due to Mr. Manson's gambling addiction, he had lost almost all his ancestral property. To him, the only solution left was his best friend from school—Richard Anderson.

Mr. Manson had brought the marriage proposal to the Anderson family for this very reason. However, sensing his true motives, both Mrs. Anderson and Isabella had been rejecting it. Andrew knew that Godfrey Manson was actually a very obedient, kind, and innocent man toward his father.

"I thought that once we rejected the proposal, Mr. Manson wouldn't come back. But he has returned... I don't know what kind of plan is brewing in his head!" Isabella said, a faint, cold smile playing on her lips. Andrew wondered if he should say something in return.

A few moments later, they were in the grand, decorated drawing room of the Anderson mansion. Mr. Manson, with his cunning face, was seated on a comfortable sofa next to Richard Anderson. Isabella greeted them and took a seat near Mrs. Anderson.

Andrew's eyes fell upon a young man and a young woman sitting in the room. Their faces bore a look of deep sorrow. Yet, in that moment, Andrew did not realize that this young woman would one day turn the lives of many—including his own—upside down. With her thick, dark hair and dark eyes, a sharp nose, and thin lips, she possessed an aura that Andrew found somewhat harsh.

"Andrew... this is Bill," Richard Anderson said, pointing to the young man. "When you go to London next month, Bill will be our driver. I want you to train him. Do you understand?"

"Yes, Master," Andrew replied, looking at Bill, who had an unassuming appearance.

"Very well, Manson... I have given Bill a job here as your assistant. But I don't have a job for this girl. She's far too young to be a maid," Richard Anderson remarked. Manson's face clouded with a sudden shadow of grief. "Oh, Anderson... you have done me a great favor this time as well. Bill is like my own child—my loyal driver who grew up with me. But as you know, my gambling habit eventually cost me even my horses. I couldn't just cast Bill aside."

"That is why I came to you. But what will happen to this poor girl, **Sarah.** She has only just turned twenty. Sara grew up in an orphanage in London. She was a great help to my wife in her final days. She was always loyal. But now, we can't even afford to pay her a wage or provide her with accommodation. What can we do? It's her misfortune...! She will have to go back to the orphanage and look for some other work."

Isabella, her heart full of sympathy, looked at Sarah. "Mother... let's take Sarah in as my maid."

Mrs. Anderson, looking troubled, glanced at her daughter. "Isabella... you already have maids. You have the head housekeeper to look after you."

"But Mother, I want her as my personal maid. It would be good for her, wouldn't it? Besides, we can afford to pay one more servant."

Andrew felt a wave of unease. He realized Isabella was doing this solely out of the kindness of her heart. However, looking at the girl's harsh expression, he truly disliked the idea of her becoming Isabella's maid.

"When I leave, Helly will serve you with the utmost dedication. There is no need for an extra wage... please, let them stay together."

"No, Andrew... Helly is my friend. She will stay in this mansion as she is. Let Sarah be my maid. That way, she will have a job too."

"Very well then..." Richard Anderson muttered. "Manson, Sarah will work as my daughter's maid..."

With those words from Richard Anderson, Andrew saw a flash of burning hatred in Sarah's eyes. For the first time, Andrew recognized a hidden cruelty within her. Yet, he remained silent, unable to grasp the true nature of what he had witnessed.

Thus, Sarah and Bill entered service at the Anderson Banglow. Bill, a young man with habitually messy hair, was always frank and spoke his mind openly. Andrew grew fond of him, and within a few days, they became close companions.

When Andrew announced his intention to return to his higher education, Helly was thrilled; however, she felt a deep sense of sorrow at the thought of being separated from her brother. Both Andrew and the young mistress, Isabella, had been trying their best to cheer Helly up.

One morning, Isabella called Helly to her room. As Helly entered, she saw Isabella showing Sarah how to cut a certain garment. Helly had noticed that Sarah did not particularly care for the mansion's staff. Nor did Sarah seem to form any close bonds with anyone. When Helly once told Isabella that she felt Sarah didn't like her, Isabella had simply laughed it off as Helly's imagination.

"Ah, Helly... come in. I've been waiting for you!" Isabella said in a joyful voice. "Look at what I've brought you from the city today..." Isabella said, handing a parcel to Helly.

Helly's eyes sparkled with delight. She hurriedly opened the package and could hardly believe what she saw. It was an exquisitely decorated hat. To keep the hat in place, there was a beautiful lace ribbon to tie under the chin. Helly's face lit up with pure happiness.

"Oh... my lady... is this really for me? Thank you so much, Oh, thank you a thousand times..." Helly said, her voice trembling with joy.

"I'm so glad you like it, Helly," Isabella replied warmly.

"My lady... you, the Master, and Mrs. Anderson treat us so kindly. I don't know how to thank you enough. After coming here, I feel like the world has become such a beautiful place... Truly, to have a mistress like you is such a blessing," Helly said.

Just as Helly finished speaking, she witnessed a shocking sight. Helly was standing in front of Isabella, while Sara was standing behind Isabella, cutting a dress. Suddenly, with a sharp movement, Sara took the scissors and sliced right through the middle of the dress. Hearing the sound of the fabric tearing, Isabella spun around.

"Oh! Oh, Miss Isabella... my hand slipped and I've ruined the dress..." Sarah said in a sweet, soft voice, though it sounded like a mere whisper.

Isabella's face darkened with sadness. It was one of her favorite outfits. "Fine, take it away and see if you can do something with it," she sighed.

As Sarah took the dress and left the room, Helly turned toward Isabella with a flushed, indignant face.

"My lady... I saw it clearly. She did it on purpose. She acted just like a great actress," Helly insisted.

"Oh, Helly, let it go. Why would she do that?" Isabella laughed. "If you had seen the way she cried when she broke the glass of my favorite photo ... ." Isabella turned away, showing Helly a small drawing. It was a pencil sketch of a young Isabella nestled against her father.

"This was drawn by a very famous artist. I told Andrew to have it framed for me..."

Helly remained silent. However, she was certain that what she had seen was no illusion.

"Oh, my dear Helly... there's no use being jealous with Sarah. After all, she can never take your place. You are my friend... Sarah is my servant. There is a difference between you two, as wide as the earth and the sky."

Helly smiled faintly. However, she felt she must tell Andrew what had happened.

Gradually, the day of Andrew's departure for London arrived. His heart grew heavy with the thought of leaving. He went to the stables to say goodbye to the horses he had cared for so lovingly. There, he found Bill.

"Hey...Andrew!" Bill called out cheerfully. "I was wondering if you'd come by here."

"Yes, I've come at just the right time," Andrew said, leaning against a wooden beam.

"Even so...I'm going to miss you, Andrew... my good friend...!" Bill said with a hint of sadness.

"But I'll come back as soon as I get a break, Bill. Look after my sister and Little Mistress Isabella well.... We owe everything to Little Mistress Isabella."

"Hmm..." Bill fell into deep thought. "I never thought she was such a kind person. She talks to the horses so gently... just like she's talking to little babies. Sometimes she looks worried, as if she's afraid of hurting their feelings. But... I think it's because of her kindness that she doesn't see the big trouble brewing right under her nose."

"Bill, what are you talking about?"

"Andrew... to be honest, I'm talking about Sarah," Bill said in a low, serious voice. He bit his lip for a moment, then looked at Andrew with a hardened expression. "I've been debating whether to tell you this for days... it's been weighing on my heart, Andrew. That's why I'm telling you now."

Andrew looked at him with wide eyes. Sarah... the girl with the cruel eyes! What did Bill know about her?

"Andrew, you know very well about Mr. Manson. It's true he was my master. But for his own gain, he is a man who would do anything..."

Manson's proposal was ultimately rejected. Consequently, he brought Sarah forward. "Who do you think Sarah is? Perhaps you don't even believe my words..." Bill began to explain the details.

Years before Mr. Richard Anderson married Mrs.Anderson, he had wed an Irish woman. However, due to some reason, the two of them separated quickly. According to Mr. Manson, that woman was very poor and possessed a volatile, harsh temperament. He claimed he had seen her attack Mr. Richard violently on several occasions.

Eventually, that woman went back to her home country. A few months later, she gave birth to a child—that child was Sarah. Though she was never officially recognized, she is Richard Anderson's firstborn. The truth is, Mr. Richard never knew a thing about this.

He had assumed the woman who came into his life had simply vanished. In reality, she had fallen ill and passed away shortly after. Manson's company had provided Richard with only that much information. Afterward, Richard moved on and started a new life.

Sarah's grandmother was unable to raise the child, so she handed her over to an orphanage in London. Two or three years ago, Sarah tracked down Mr. Manson. Around that time, Manson's name was in the newspapers—described as a "corrupt businessman who destroyed properties for money."

Despite this, Sarah went to him. Manson himself hadn't known of her existence. However, Sarah's grandmother had given her old wedding photographs and mentioned that a man named 'Manson' was a friend of her father, Richard.

That is how Sarah found him. Her initial intention was simply to find Richard and claim the inheritance she felt she was owed. But that day, Manson turned her away. He knew that if Richard found out, it would lead to a massive scandal.

But then... when Manson's proposal was rejected, he changed his strategy. He decided to bring Sarah into the fold. If he could prove she was Richard's daughter, she would be entitled to a large portion of the property. Then, Manson could marry his son to Sarah and reclaim his wealth.

Andrew stood there, stunned into silence. If he hadn't known Bill's character so well, he wouldn't have believed a word of it. But he had to consider it seriously. He looked at Isabella, who was watching Sarah with a look of pure hatred.

The situation felt like a knot that couldn't be untied. Because of a "vile girl" like Sarah, the entire Anderson family was on the verge of ruin. Andrew looked at Bill and sighed.

"I don't understand, Bill! What am I supposed to do?"

"I don't understand either, Andrew... but you know Sarah trusts me. Out of everyone here, I'm the only one who knows her true nature. Sarah came to me in a hurry today and said if she doesn't get what she wants, she's going to tell Mr. Anderson everything tomorrow. That is the worst thing that could happen!"

Andrew's eyes grew red as he looked toward the dark garden. "The best thing to do is to talk to her one more time. I must stop her from destroying the Anderson family, no matter what."

"Bill, can you bring her here?"

"Andrew, I will try. I'll try to change her mind. But I don't have much faith in it. Regardless of what happens, I love the Anderson family. I won't let Sarah destroy their happiness."

Bill walked toward the mansion with a heavy heart, leaving Andrew alone in the darkness of the stable. If Isabella had not felt sympathy for Sarah that day, Sarah may never get a chance to create any problems.

A lantern flickered in the distance, casting light toward the stable. Andrew saw Sarah's silhouette approaching. Her face was filled with a cold curiosity. A moment later, she stood in front of him.

"So... Andrew... Bill told me you wanted to talk to me," she said, her voice dry and mocking.

"About what...?"

"Sarah... I want to talk to you about you. I know the truth about you."

"Oh...? So Bill told you about me...!" She bit her lip with sudden aggression. "Well, it doesn't matter. Everyone will find out soon anyway."

Sarah let out a cold, cynical laugh.

"No, Sarah... don't do that. This isn't something that should ever happen."

"Oh, Andrew... the 'faithful driver' of the Anderson family! Yes, you've certainly gained a lot by serving them. Aren't you going to London the day after tomorrow? Don't be afraid. By the time you return, this beautiful mansion will belong to me,You might not even be able to set foot in here again!"

"No, Sarah... listen to me. Be patient. You can't do this! You can't force yourself on Mr. Anderson like this."

"Patient?!" Sarah screamed in a rage. "I've already been patient for twenty years! I suffered in an orphanage for fifteen years!"

"At fifteen, I learned everything about my parents from my grandmother. But she didn't know where they were! Finally, she died. I suffered everywhere, doing every kind of job... while Isabella enjoyed all the luxury that was meant for me! I suffered alone!"

"You are thinking about this the wrong way!" Andrew replied, his own anger rising. "No one else is to blame for your misfortunes!"

Sarah's eyes burned with an uncontrollable malice. Seeing that look, Andrew's heart sank.

"I am Richard Anderson's first child! But I never got what I should deserve. Yet Isabella gets everything—more than she even deserves! Then what about me...? I have been a slave to her! Should I remain a slave to her for even a moment longer? No... I won't wait anymore...! I will reclaim my rights!"

Andrew spoke with a firm resolve. Without a second glance, Sarah left the room with a swift, arrogant stride. Andrew watched her go, unable to say a word. Suddenly, a rustling sound came from the bushes near the stable, and a moment later, a shadow emerged from the foliage.

"Andrew..." Helly's voice was trembling.

Andrew was startled. "My God... Helly...!"

For a moment, they both stood there, staring at one another in silence.

"What can we do now, Andrew?"

"There is nothing for us to do, Helly... we can only wait. If we tell Isabella everything, she will take the right steps... but until then, we must remain silent, Helli."

"Yes... Andrew... I can't even imagine someone like Sarah being Isabella's half-sister! I don't know how this will end... if Sarah hadn't come here, how much good things would have been!"

Andrew sighed deeply and turned his gaze toward the lonely, dark night.

The next morning, Helly moved all her belongings from her small hut to the room reserved for her at the mansion.

Andrew, meanwhile, packed his things into a trunk, preparing for his journey to London. Since he was to leave for the station with Bill the following day, Andrew moved his belongings into Bill's room at the mansion. As he looked back at his small house, Isabella walked over to him.

"What is it, Andrew...?"

"I can't even think straight, Miss... everything happened so fast. In this small house, we spent days in sorrow and pain. You came into our lives like an angel and brought us happiness..."

Isabella smiled softly, a look of kindness in her eyes. Andrew was deeply moved. He had never seen her treat anyone with anything but kindness. He wondered how she would manage this difficult situation with Sarah.

"We will miss you very much, Andrew... That's why you must finish your degree quickly. One day, you will be a brilliant man. You will be famous... and then I will say with pride, 'See that man? He is my friend.' But Andrew, will you say, 'Who is this crazy girl? I've never seen her before'?"

They both laughed out loud.

"Miss, do you really think I would ever be such a person...?"

"No, Andrew... you aren't like that... but you have every right to be proud," Isabella said, smiling.

"But in my mind, I have a beautiful vision of what our future will be like... My dear friend Helly will become a great lady and live in a beautiful house... and on her way, she will tell her children the stories I told her... In the spring, I will go to her house to have tea with her. And by then... you! You will be a professor at a university like Cambridge or Oxford, wearing big glasses, buried under piles of books...! Your wife will bring you tea, and you won't even have time to drink it...!"

Andrew couldn't help but laugh at the vivid picture she painted. Isabella joined in.

"Miss... you've made up such a lovely story... but I think you'll be a world-famous writer...!"

"Yes... perhaps...! Whatever happens, our lives will be very happy! So Andrew, I must go now... tomorrow morning Helly and I will come to the station to see you off. Until you return, I will look after Helly like my own sister..."

"I have no doubt about that, Miss... thank you so much..."

Isabella gave him a sweet smile and walked away. However, as the next morning approached, Andrew couldn't help but worry about the tension Sarah had brought into the mansion.

That night, before going to sleep, Isabella talked to Helly.

"Helly... I know you are very sad about Andrew leaving... but don't be sad... think of it as having someone else to stay with you instead of your brother. He looked after you with so much love for fifteen years... I can never take his place. But a separation from a friend like Andrew is painful for me too... regardless, I am here for you, Helly. My parents will be yours too. This will be your home..."

Isabella took Helly's hand with great affection. Tears welled up in Helly's eyes. Isabella had always been her heroine, but in that moment, she felt a bond as deep as a sisterhood.

"My lady... I am in this beautiful mansion, wearing these beautiful clothes, only because of you... I only ask one thing of you. Please let me look after you and your family as your companion... nothing would bring me more happiness. Then I can be by your side forever..."

Isabella smiled. "For now, you can stay here with us as part of the family, Helly... and one day, you will have an even better life..."

That night at the Anderson mansion, Andrew had to stay in Bill's room until morning. But sleep did not come easily to him even as midnight passed. After dinner, he had seen Sarah walking toward Mr. Anderson's study room. Tomorrow was going to be a day of great change. He wondered how Mr. Anderson would receive his first daughter after all these years.

It was a very warm summer night. Andrew paced the room, feeling a sense of unease. It was already past two in the morning.

Suddenly, the sound of someone pounding hardly on their door echoed through the room.

"Hurry up... Andrew... Bill... wake up quickly!" It was Hallie's voice.

Andrew opened the door immediately. He saw Bill, who had just woken up, rubbing his eyes and looking on in confusion.

"Helly... what is this?" Andrew asked anxiously.

"Bill, go and bring the doctor quickly! Mr. Anderson is unconscious. He has fallen in the study room!"

In an instant, Bill grabbed his coat and rushed out to find the doctor, while Helly and Andrew ran toward the study room.

"What happened, Helly?" Andrew asked urgently.

"I don't know, Andrew... I woke up after the servants started screaming."

As they entered the study room, they saw Mrs. Anderson and several servants already there. Mrs. Anderson's face was deathly pale. The servants were whispering to one another; among their murmurs, the word "dead" could be heard time and again.

They had lifted Mr. Anderson and placed him on the sofa. However, the moment Andrew saw his still, lifeless body, he realized he was gone. When the doctor arrived, he confirmed the tragic conclusion: Mr. Anderson had passed away due to a heart attack.

The doctor concluded that the death had occurred more than three hours prior. Andrew felt as though his world was collapsing. While Mrs. Anderson began to wail in grief, Helly stood staring blankly, making no effort to wipe away the tears streaming down her face. Andrew gently took his sister's hand.

"This happened because of her, Andrew... this happened because Sarah revealed the truth," Helly whispered hoarsely.

Andrew unknowingly tightened his grip on her hand. Whether there was not Isabella or Sarah, but whenever Isabella found out the truth was bound to suffer—this was the thought that crossed both Andrew and Hallie's minds.

As the servants led the weeping Mrs. Anderson out of the room, Andrew, holding his grieving sister's hand, walked out of that painful chamber. But they were not prepared for the even more agonizing event that was about to unfold.

Bill ran toward Andrew with a face as white as a paper.

"Andrew... I... I went to the stable to get the horse... and Andrew... through the rows of trees, I saw a bright light... your house! Andrew... your house is on fire!"

Andrew and Helly looked at each other, stunned. In an instant, they were standing in front of their small house, watching the flames roar toward the dark sky. Bill and several others were desperately trying to extinguish the fire, while Hallie covered her face with her hands.

"What is happening? No... these things shouldn't be happening, Andrew... I can't even think anymore..."

Andrew stood like a statue, silent. As the fire spread, the surroundings began to glow with an eerie light.

Suddenly, a young man who had been trying to douse the flames screamed. others ran toward him. Andrew and Helly rushed there as well. When Andrew saw the horrific sight, his entire body went numb. Hallie fainted and fell to the ground.

Before them lay the lifeless body of Isabella, her skin charred and burnt to a dark hue!

Yes! Truly, on that terrible night, Isabella too had departed from this world… It was not a natural death; she had been brutally murdered by someone. The post-mortem revealed that she had been killed by a heavy blow to the head inside the small house before it was set on fire.

The police began an investigation. Yet, even as they searched for clues, the beloved young heiress of the mansion had been murdered in cold blood. Mrs. Anderson, already broken by her husband's death, lost her sanity completely upon seeing her only daughter's charred body. She was soon taken to a mental hospital.

All the servants left the mansion, claiming it was a cursed place. Rumors spread through the village that the curse of Helly had caused this destruction. The villagers believed that since Helly's parents had died in a fire, Isabella had met the same fate due to the dark influence surrounding Helly's soul.

Mr. Anderson's body was buried in the churchyard, but Isabella's body was left aside, as people feared to touch "the one who died under a curse."

No one from the village came to the funeral. Only Andrew, Helly, and Bill remained in the empty mansion. Bill eventually left, unable to stay any longer, leaving Andrew and Helly alone.

Together, Andrew and Helly buried Isabella's body beneath the Oak tree in the small hill, where Helly and Isabella met at first day.

Chapter 11

Rooted deeper than soil

Finally, everything fell silent. The greatest pain is felt not by those who leave, but by those left behind to live with the memories. Andrew and Helly lived through that agony. The mental toll was so great that it felt as though there was no more room for sorrow in the world.

They couldn't even think about going back to the village. The villagers looked at Helly as if she were a ghost. It was Bill who brought them food from the village out of pity.

Helly, dressed in tattered clothes, spent her days sitting by Isabella's grave. She had no joy, no hope, and no purpose left in life. Just as Isabella had entered their lives so suddenly, she had vanished just as fast.

As time passed, Helly's appearance changed. She became as pale as a ghost, her eyes sunken into her skull. She suffered from constant, severe headaches. Eventually, Helly became bedridden. Andrew, witnessing all this pain, tried his best to help his sister, but she had no desire to live. Her courage had vanished.

One day, she called out to Andrew. "Andrew... they... haven't they found them yet?"

Andrew gently stroked his sister's head. "Found what, Helly? What are you talking about?"

"The police... haven't they found the people who killed my lady Isabella?"

"No, Hallie... my sister... don't think about those things. Be a good girl and get well soon."

Helly let out a deep, sorrowful sigh.

"Andrew... why did you do that, Andrew? Why didn't you just let me die in the fire when I was born? You and parents were living so happily. I came into your world and made your lives miserable... and then, later, I ruined everything. Because of me, your life was destroyed, Andrew... Why did you save my life?"

"Oh, for God's sake, Helly... stop talking this way..Please…When my mother and father died, I comforted myself by thinking that I still had a sister of my own in this world. Didn't you ever know that, Helly? If there was one bond that made me want to live in this world, it was you...

you were my little sister. Except for you, I have respected and loved no one else but Miss Isabella. She left us in such a painful way, but I still have you, my little sister... In this world, even if I lose everything, you are worth more to me than my own life."

As tears welled in Helly's eyes, she placed his hands over Andrew’s and squeezed them tight.

"Andrew... we are so unfortunate. But... but... I can only find peace when I see justice being served for Miss Isabella. Only then, Andrew. I believe... the little mistress always trusted in nature... justice will surely be served one day, Andrew. We were waiting for that, Andrew. We cannot live apart from her memory."

"Yes, certainly,Helly. As long as there is god, justice will surely be served. But we must have the patience to wait for it."

Days passed. Andrew firmly believed that Sarah was responsible for everything that had happened. Even thinking about Isabella's death made his heart burn with anger.

Finally, that decisive day arrived. Andrew, who had been sitting by the bed in a state of deep sorrow, had just finished feeding Helly. Just then, unexpectedly, Sarah entered the room! She was adorned in magnificent clothes and jewelry.

"Andrew... are you still in this mansion?" Sara's voice echoed with contempt. "How are you all still here?"

"Sarah... you are a truly wicked girl!" Andrew roared in anger. "Because of you, the entire Anderson family was destroyed."

"Oh, oh Andrew...Yeah.. I destroyed it! I destroyed the Anderson family!" Sara laughed mockingly.

"Andrew... do you know what happened that night? You must be dying to know, aren't you? I went to meet my father-Richard Anderson. When I told him about myself, he didn't believe me at first. But I had their wedding photos—my mother's photos. After seeing how much I looked like my mother, Anderson was shocked."

"He just stared at me. Then he suddenly clutched the left side of his chest tightly. After that, he collapsed. When I went close to look, he wasn't breathing. I felt like I was finally loosing everything again which I should deserved back from Isabella. I went to her room and woke that innocent Isabella! I told her that Andrew had suddenly called her to come home. I told her to hurry and take a shortcut through the small house of Andrew. She believed me... as soon as she went into your house, the blow I struck killed her instantly! After that, I burnt all the house using kerosene..."

Before Sarah could finish, Andrew jumped forward and grabbed Sarah, locking him in a tight embrace. Sara began to wail loudly. At that moment, amidst the sounds of Helly's crying, heavy footsteps echoed, and police officers burst into Andrew's room!

The police officers who entered the room immediately handcuffed Andrew's hands. Behind them, Mr. Manson entered the room.

"Now do you see, gentlemen... how these low-lifes get agitated when their secrets are caught?" Mr. Manson said with a cold, triumphant smile.

"What is this... what are you talking about? Why are you putting handcuffs on my hands?" Andrew shouted in shock.

One police officer spoke in a harsh voice. "We are taking you into custody in connection with the death of Isabella Anderson. We found the blood-stained iron rod used for the murder hidden in your suitcase!"

"Oh my God... what are you saying? This Sarah... she just said she killed her!" Andrew screamed in rage.

"We will have to see about that in court... hmm... let's go now."

Bill suddenly ran into the room. Unable to understand what was happening, he was consumed by a fierce anger.

"This is a mistake! Andrew is innocent! That night, he was in my room... this cannot be!"

"Fine, come to court and testify! For now, we are taking him."

Andrew looked at Helly with helpless eyes. Terrified, she watched the proceedings in silence. Tears began to stream down Andrew's cheeks.

"In the name of God, Bill... look after her. Please... take care of my sister!" Andrew could only manage to say that much.

After several months, Andrew sat within the four walls of a prison cell—an innocent man imprisoned for a crime he did not commit. He spent the nights in agony, his cries of pain echoing through the prison walls.

****

Anne wiped the tears falling down her cheeks and sighed. she looked at the elderly Andrew with immense pain.

"How much have you suffered, Andrew? What happened after that?"

Andrew slowly closed both his eyes.

"Little lady… after Bill provided the evidence for my sake, I was forced to spend three years in prison. On the very day the police took me away, my poor Helly passed away. After enduring so much pain, she finally took her leave today... Bill has buried my dear sister Helly behind those trees, right beside Miss Isabella." Andrew spoke these words through her tears.

Old Andrew then went to fetch a tattered mat. Placing it over the cold stones, he sat down with great difficulty, his fingers tracing some faded markings scratched into the surface.

HELLY — 1819

"Bill never knew that which year Helly was born. But my friend Bill did everything he could for her until the very end. When I was released from prison, I went straight to Bill's house. Even though I was free because of his testimony, we didn't have enough strong evidence to bring charges against Sarah. Regardless, I stayed here as their head servant… all I wanted was to see justice for little lady Isabella and Helly."

Mr.Manson had orchestrated a marriage between his son, Godfrey Manson, and Sarah to secure the property. But fate had a different plan—one no one could have predicted.

Sarah gained nothing. There was no evidence to prove she was Mr. Anderson's daughter. Consequently, the bungalow passed to the son of Mr. Richard's brother-Your father - Jonathan Anderson! I originally came here to work in the gardens because of him. Yet, he gave Sarah the position of head housekeeper. The number of times I thought of killing her is beyond measure… but every time I saw little lady Isabella's innocent face, I stopped myself. I waited. Sarah Manson received nothing, and later, Godfrey Manson passed away. Your father always lived in fear of Sarah. He felt that all this property belonged to her."

Sarah had a dream—to see her daughter inherit the estate. But if you had died that day, the last of the Andersons would have vanished, and everything would have fallen under Sarah Manson's control. Justice might never have been served.

But Helly came back for her friend! Finally, justice was done. After all these years, Helly's soul has finally found peace through saving your life."Andrew let out a long, soft sigh and offered a faint smile.

After death of Sarah Manson, her daughter Lily left for a nunnery. Andrew who had spent last years of his life in peace, passed away quietly a few months later. In accordance with his final wish, his remains were buried by the villagers in the same grave area next to Helly and Isabella.

Ultimately, Anne lived in this world alongside the memories of those two- Andrew and Helly. Yet, she believed that one day, in some other life, the three of them would meet again and find the happiness that eluded them here.

*********** THE END. **************

www.ingramcontent.com/pod-product-compliance
Ingram Content Group UK Ltd.
Pitfield, Milton Keynes, MK11 3LW, UK
UKHW021409190726
13845UKWH00028B/977

9 789357 172394